WINNER OF

The 2000 Alberta Playwriting Competition
The 2002 Betty Mitchell Award for Outstanding New Play
The 2003 Gwen Pharis Ringwood Award for Drama,
Alberta Literary Awards

PRAISE FOR *Mary's Wedding*

"There are many thrills that can be experienced in the theater. But the sensation of flying through a landscape on the back of a galloping horse is not usually among them. So there's a certain bravado . . . in writing a play about a cavalry charge. Or about lovers whose feelings ripen on horseback. In *Mary's Wedding* . . . Stephen Massicotte gets us up in the saddle for both."
—*The New York Times*

"[L]ove and war may be the oldest stories we have. But they also never grow old, especially not when they are told with as much delicacy and restraint as Massicotte's play displays . . . "
—*The Boston Globe*

"Put[s] you in mind of the grand passion of Catherine and Heathcliff in *Wuthering Heights*, the vastness of their love mirroring the wild tangle of nature." —*The Washington Times*

"You can tell from the audience's rapt silence that this is a special show, not to be missed." —*NOW Magazine*, Toronto

"[T]aps into some strikingly intense feelings about love, loss, and recovery." —*Chicago Tribune*

"*Mary's Wedding* . . . proves Massicotte is a gifted storyteller with an ear for detail and imagery. . . . It was Massicotte's descriptive writing that allowed the audience to really lose themselves in the moment. There was nary a dry eye in the house by the time the actors took their final bows." —*Calgary Herald*

"Spare, artful, ethereal, powerful, and unexpectedly poetic . . . the tale is written with such freshness, invention, and emotional depth that it's anything but predictable."
—*Journal Sentinel*, Milwaukee, WI

"The opening-night audience sat entranced and the final moments are some of the most heart wrenching I have experienced in a theatre in a long time." —*Edmonton Sun*

"With a refreshing lack of cynicism, this deeply romantic dream-play goes straight to the heart with timely themes of love and loss during wartime." —*The Seattle Times*

"*Mary's Wedding* has audiences breathing in at the first words and only consciously exhaling after the last scene ends."
—*Victoria Rainbow News*

"[A] ninety-minute experience through heartbreaking surreality."
—*Indianapolis Examiner*

"Both poignant and suspenseful, the play is relevant to this day."
—*CurtainUp*, Los Angeles

"Covering first love thwarted by war, how loving someone strongly is as frightening as it is exhilarating, and companionship in war, the play's dream setting now in this revival achieves full effect."
—*Edinburgh Guide*

"Stephen Massicotte is the poet, working with homey materials to create a 95-minute love story. . . . It turns the audience into poets, too, making us imaginative participants in this story of doomed love."—*Pittsburgh Post-Gazette*

"Massicotte doesn't push his anti-war message. He doesn't have to. The charm of his romance juxtaposed against prosaic descriptions from the trenches . . . do it for him."
—*San Francisco Chronicle*

"[T]he way the playwright works with the dream structure he's set up is skilled and subtle. It just works so well."
—*Regina Reviews*

"A play that understands loving and grieving and shakes you with the horrible immediacy of war."—*Orlando Sentinel*

"This is what theatre is about. A brilliantly written piece reflecting true to heart relationships and what is needed to be done to work through obstacles to reach the one you love."
—*Chicago Stage Standard*

"Massicotte's play is simple, too—deceptively so, in that its uncomplicated story contains a world of experience."
—*Washington City Paper*

"Have you ever had a dream so real you wish it could be true? *Mary's Wedding* is like that dream; sublime and thoughtful, it lingers in your mind long after you've woken up and gone home."
—*Avenue Calgary*

"Massicotte writes with an earnestness that is rare in this cynical day and age." —*San Jose Mercury News*

"The truth is in the details, and Massicotte's lovely language is well-grounded, but aspires to its own sort of poetry. It doesn't overshoot the mark. . . . The narration is vivid, but the relationship between the young lovers, Mary and Charlie, is rendered in charming, everyday exchanges." —*Milwaukee Magazine*

"Massicotte blends a war story that could well be a two-act action play, and the story of two lovers intriguing enough to be a two-act conventional romance, into a one-act tightly constructed play, but never seems to be slighting either story." —*Potomac Stages*, Washington, DC

"[T]he tale is genuinely affecting." —*TimeOut*, Chicago

"Lightning strikes fast and hard before soldier boy Charlie and local girl Mary have even met in Stephen Massicotte's gorgeous little First World War–set two-hander. . . . Massicotte mines a similar vein of magic and loss in a cruel world to create this heartfelt elegy to love and war." —*Herald Scotland*

"The ending really is quite extraordinary in its emotional impact."
—CBC Radio Canada

MARY'S WEDDING

ALSO BY STEPHEN MASSICOTTE

The Clockmaker
The Oxford Roof Climber's Rebellion

MARY'S WEDDING

Stephen Massicotte

PLAYWRIGHTS CANADA PRESS
Toronto

LIBRARY AND ARCHIVES CANADA CATALOGUING IN PUBLICATION
Massicotte, Stephen, author
     Mary's wedding / Stephen Massicotte. -- Third edition.

A play.
Issued in print and electronic formats.
ISBN 978-1-77091-542-8 (paperback).--ISBN 978-1-77091-543-5 (pdf).--
ISBN 978-1-77091-544-2 (html).--ISBN 978-1-77091-545-9 (mobi)

     I. Title.

PS8576.A79668M37 2016   C812'.6   C2016-900215-2
                                                 C2016-900216-0

Playwrights Canada Press operates on Mississaugas of the Credit, Wendat, Anishinaabe, Métis, and Haudenosaunee land. It always was and always will be Indigenous land.

We acknowledge the financial support of the Canada Council for the Arts—which last year invested $153 million to bring the arts to Canadians throughout the country—the Ontario Arts Council (OAC), Ontario Creates, and the Government of Canada for our publishing activities.

Canada Council
for the Arts
Conseil des arts
du Canada

ONTARIO ARTS COUNCIL
CONSEIL DES ARTS DE L'ONTARIO
an Ontario government agency
un organisme du gouvernement de l'Ontario

Canada

ONTARIO | ONTARIO
CREATES | CRÉATIF

For Robin

HISTORICAL NOTE

Lt. Gordon Muriel Flowerdew. Photos courtesy of LdSH (RC), Regimental Museum and Archives.

Lieutenant Gordon Muriel Flowerdew was awarded the Victoria Cross for leading C Squadron, the Lord Strathcona's Horse (Royal Canadians), in a charge at Moreuil Wood on March 30, 1918. He died of his wounds on March 31, at No. 41 Casualty Clearing Station. He is buried at Namps-au-Val British Cemetery, France, eleven miles southwest of Amiens. Plot I. Row H. Grave 1. The first day of rehearsal for the first production of this play took place on January 2, 2002. This was the 117th anniversary of his birthday.

The following letter was postmarked in the field on the day that he died, and arrived in England on April 4, 1918.

Letter from Lt. Gordon Muriel Flowerdew to his mother. Letter courtesy of LdSH (RC), Regimental Museum and Archives.

My dearest Mother,

Have been a bit busy lately, so haven't been able to write. I managed to borrow this card. Haven't had any mail for some days, so we are very keen to see the papers. The weather is still very good, but very keen at night— Have had the most wonderful experiences lately and wouldn't have missed it for anything— Best love to all.

Your affectionate son,
Gordon

*Collin Doyle and Sarah M. Smith in the 2002 Alberta Theatre Projects
production. Photos by HarderLee Photography.*

Mary's Wedding was first produced in February 2002 by Alberta Theatre Projects at the Enbridge playRites Festival of New Canadian Plays in Calgary, Alberta, with the following cast and creative crew:

Charlie: Collin Doyle
Mary/Flowers: Sarah M. Smith

Director: Gina Wilkinson
Set Designer: Scott Reid
Costume Designer: David Boechler
Lighting Designer: Melinda Sutton
Composer/Sound Designer: Bob Doble
Festival Dramaturge: Vanessa Porteous
Assistant Dramaturge: Vicki Stroich
Production Stage Manager: Dianne Goodman
Stage Manager: Crystal Beatty
Assistant Stage Manager: Karen Fleury
University of Calgary Intern: Angela Bewick

The play was remounted for a tenth anniversary production by Alberta Theatre Projects from March 27 through April 14, 2012, with the following cast and creative team:

Charlie: Alessandro Juliani
Mary/Flowers: Meg Roe

Director: Bob White
Set Designer: Narda McCarroll
Lighting Designer: Narda McCarroll
Sound Designer: Matthew Waddell

Alessandro Juliani and Meg Roe in the 2012 Alberta Theatre Projects production. Photos by HarderLee Photography.

CHARACTERS

Charlie
Mary
Flowers

For a while, in the deep blue-and-green darkness, the sound of a light breeze can be heard. CHARLIE emerges from the shadows.

CHARLIE Hello, out there. Thank you for coming. Before we begin there is something I have to tell you.

Tonight is the night before Mary's wedding. It's a July wedding on a Saturday morning in nineteen hundred and twenty; two years after the end of the Great War, or as you might know it now, the First World War.

So, tomorrow is Mary's wedding, tonight is just a dream. I ask you to remember that. It begins at the end and ends at the beginning. There are sad parts.

Don't let that stop you from dreaming it too.

A barefoot girl in a nightgown enters.

MARY It always starts the same. I dream it is dawn, in a field. I'm in my wedding dress. I'm out there looking for flowers for my bouquet. It is a quiet and peaceful morning.

Then I see someone walking through the grass. At first he is no one in particular, just a figure walking, but then I see that I know him. He has a face I know well.

He smiles and I follow his eyes to a horse sleeping in the damp grass. She wakes from her dream and stands up. He steps by her neck and shoulder and touches and calms her. It has been a long, cold night but the morning sun warms them.

That's when it starts to rain, slowly at first, then heavier and heavier. He and his horse don't move and I always wonder why. It's raining very hard and they should find some shelter, a tree, or a barn . . . somewhere, but they don't. He just stands there, looking up into the rainstorm, getting ready to count the thousands from the flash to the rumble.

I call to them. They never hear me but I call to them anyway. RUN, CHARLIE, RUN! PLEASE! Ride away from there! Get in from the storm! But they can't hear me. They never hear me. They just stand very still.

Then, just before a white flash like lightning cuts them into sharp outline, he says something I cannot make out.

CHARLIE . . .

MARY   Then it goes dark.

A flash and darkness.

And before the words Charlie says form into under-standing in my head . . . there is thunder.

Thunder. A rain falls outside an old barn.

When I can see again, I am running down the turn in the road, down from the bridge, into the old barn. This is years ago. It's a downpour and I've been caught in it. I'm soaking wet. I'm late. Mother will be worried.

Inside, it smells of wood, old rope, and . . . horse.

CHARLIE and his horse are in the barn staring upward, as they were in the field. Outside, a thunderstorm approaches with a far-off flash of lightning.

CHARLIE   One-one thousand, two-one thousand, three-one thousand, four-one thousand, five-one thousand—

Thunder rumbles.

MARY   Was that just five?

CHARLIE   Shhh!

Pause.

MARY Is it coming closer?

CHARLIE What does it sound like?

MARY You're more frightened than your horse is.

CHARLIE What makes you think I'm afraid?

> *Lightning flashes closer. CHARLIE flinches.*

MARY / Oh, nothing at all—

CHARLIE One-one thousand, two-one thousand, three-one thousand, four-one thous—

> *Thunder.*

/ Shit!

MARY That was closer!

> *MARY laughs.*

Oh.

CHARLIE I'm sorry, I swear too much. I'm trying to quit. It's coming closer.

MARY I hope so. I love thunderstorms.

CHARLIE   I'm not afraid . . . I just don't like getting caught out in the rain so much.

MARY   Only the rain? You're not a bit frightened of the thunder and lightning?

CHARLIE   No . . . well, a little bit. When I was six, a tree in the schoolyard got hit by lightning. It sounded like a whip crack right beside your ear. We all jumped out of our seats. Mister MacKenzie, our teacher, had been reading "The Charge of the Light Brigade" to us. When he jumped, he threw the book.

MARY   He didn't.

CHARLIE   A kid in the third desk got hit in the back of the head—

MARY   Really?

CHARLIE   Yes, sir, with Tennyson.

MARY smiles.

Flash! Bang! It hit the tree out in the yard. Split the branch with the swing. Scorched it right off.

MARY looks doubtful.

The branch was this big around.

MARY laughs.

Well, what if you were in that swing? If that lightning had hit you? You wouldn't laugh then. Ha, ha.

MARY   Of course not, but you weren't hit, were you? The chances of you being in that swing in that rainstorm at that exact moment are very small. Almost impossible—

Lightning flashes.

CHARLIE   One-one thousand, two-one thousand, thr—

Thunder.

Shh . . . shh . . . easy there. Easy. See? Horses know.

MARY   It's coming closer, then it'll pass. There's nothing to be frightened about.

CHARLIE   Yes, there is.

MARY   Only if you mind getting a little wet.

A close bolt of lightning flashes.

CHARLIE   One-one thou—

Thunder claps almost simultaneously with the lightning. CHARLIE is visibly shaken.

MARY   Shh, shh, it's going to be all right. Just a bit more and it will be over. Shh, shh, do you know what? Whenever I'm afraid, I just talk to myself.

CHARLIE   Talk to yourself?

MARY   Sometimes I sing a song, or I recite a poem—a part of something I can remember—and everything turns out fine. Do you know any poems?

CHARLIE   "The Charge of the Light Brigade"?

MARY   How does it go?

CHARLIE   I don't remember all of it.

Lightning flashes.

MARY   / I'll help you.

CHARLIE   One-one thousand—

Thunder.

MARY   "Half a league . . ."

CHARLIE   "Half a league, half a league forward—"

MARY   "Onward."

CHARLIE   Onward, right . . .

"All in the valley of Death,
Rode the six hundred.
'Onward, the Light Brigade—'"

MARY   "Forward."

CHARLIE   " 'Forward, the Light Brigade!'
'Charge for the guns!' he said:
Into the valley of Death
Rode the six hundred."

Lightning flashes.

MARY   " 'Forward, the Light Brigade!'
Was there a man dismay'd?"

Thunder.

BOTH   "Not tho' the soldier knew
Someone had blunder'd:
Theirs not to make reply,
Theirs not to reason why,
Theirs but to do and die.
Into the valley of Death
Rode the six hundred."

A flicker of lightning.

One-one thousand, two-one thousand, three-one thousand, four-one thousand, five—

A fading roll of thunder sounds.

MARY   See?

CHARLIE   It's going away.

MARY   They always do. Well. .

BOTH   What's your name?

Sorry.

MARY   Mary Chalmers.

CHARLIE   I'm Charles Edwards. Charlie, really.

MARY   Nice to meet you, Charlie Edwards.

CHARLIE   I don't know you. I mean, I've lived here all my life and I know most everybody. I don't think I've ever seen—met you before.

MARY   My mother and I just arrived here to join my father.

CHARLIE   Where from?

MARY   From England. "To live with the colonists in the wilds
            of the Canadas," as Mother puts it. We crossed the
            Atlantic on a liner.

CHARLIE   I've never seen the ocean. What was it like?

MARY   Blue.

CHARLIE   I thought that it might be . . . blue.

MARY   I still dream of it sometimes.

CHARLIE   You dream a lot?

MARY   Oh, all the time, the most lovely dreams.

CHARLIE   Me too.

MARY   What are yours about?

CHARLIE   Oh, I don't know. Barns. Not quite as exciting as cross-
            ing the ocean.

MARY   Oh, I think barns are very exciting. They're all the rage
            in London.

            The last sounds of the rain have faded.

            The storm has gone. Mmm, I love the smell after a rain.

CHARLIE   That I do like.

MARY Well, then, I guess we can go.

CHARLIE There's no sense hiding out in here all night.

MARY Yes. Oh, I'm so late. Mother will think I've run off and joined the Suffragettes.

CHARLIE I could give you a ride home. We'll have you there in no time.

MARY It's not that far.

CHARLIE There's plenty of room for the both of us.

MARY I shouldn't really.

CHARLIE Are you afraid of something?

MARY He swings the barn door open and the sky is sunset blue clear with one bright star and more coming. The smell of trees and grass after a rain pushes the stuffy barn away.

    Charlie seems to change. He reaches with his arms and puts his foot into the stirrup and pulls himself up. He is now ten feet tall above me.

CHARLIE Are you coming up? Take my hand.

    MARY takes CHARLIE's hand. The stars bloom as they fill up the sky.

MARY   I'm up in the saddle. I can't do anything but move closer to him.

CHARLIE   Hold on, Mary. You'll be home soon.

MARY   The long blades of grass blend together and blur. The fence posts smudge as they rise up and by. One, two, three four five-six. A bird flashes across our path. His wings flicker three times and he pushes himself, flicker three times and we're gone by him.

The evening air has turned to wind as our horse's hooves drum out and splash through puddles in the road. Charlie's horse breathes as she runs. In out, in out, hish-ah, hish-ah, hish-ah. Her hooves thunder and pound and splash, thunder and splash right onto the hollow wood of the bridge. The bridge goes by with a deep brown rumble. Then splash on the other side.

Hish-ah, hish-ah, hish-ah.

I think it is fear that I am feeling. At least, I think it's fear—the speed, the noise. Breathing and thundering, with this boy that was terrified and hiding one moment and fearless and flying with me the next. Fearless and flying with me, body to body beside him.

And when I finally know that what I'm feeling is not fear but something new . . . when I finally have an idea that what I am feeling is something entirely different . . . Charlie is already gone. And I am walking up

the thirty stones to Mother's front door. I am walking
the thirty wet stones and my heart is still breathing
and thundering as fast as a charge. And my feet, my
feet are carrying me as slowly as a snail.

That night, I dream only of Charlie. I hear church bells.
I dream of white dresses, flowers, and little babies and
Charlie is there for all of it. I see him with horses. I
see him running with them, riding, in fields, in forests,
in evenings, and in mornings. I see him riding and
smiling down to the sea.

I see him on an ocean liner. I am watching him sail
away. The war is on and the Canadians are sailing for
England, then France, and, before long, the heart of
Germany.

CHARLIE I can't believe it. We are finally joining the fight. Me,
Trooper Edwards, 1st Troop, C Squadron, the Lord
Strathcona's Horse Regiment.

 They wave goodbye on the wharf.

MARY The strange thing is, I was never here. I was at home,
in my room.

 Crowds cheer and a marching band plays.

I was never here with the people on the shore. This is
not how we said goodbye. When Charlie sailed, I was
two days away by train.

Oh, but it's like a great big birthday party. The sun is shining. The Saint Lawrence is glittering. There are children waving and babies in mothers' arms. All those arms and voices.

The sound of the ocean rises and a ship's horn sounds.

CHARLIE   Thirty thousand men, seven thousand horses, on thirty-eight ocean liners. What'll they do when they see us coming?

MARY   The bands and pipes play across the waves and the men on the decks all wave back.

CHARLIE   Look at that! Isn't that something?

MARY   I'll see you, Charlie!

CHARLIE   I'll charge the Germans for you. Remember me, and before long I'll be home.

BOTH   Hooray, hooray, hooray!

CHARLIE   I'll see you, Mary! I'll be home soon!

MARY   / I'm going to marry that boy.

CHARLIE   I'm going to marry that girl.

"Dear Mary . . .

"The weather has been good every day out of the Saint Lawrence. Someone 'volunteered' 1st Troop to make the crossing on the ship with the horses. Every inch of the boat is filled with them, so they've got us sleeping up on deck in hammocks."

MARY   The ships move like ghosts, steadily humming through the Atlantic. They're not pretty white like I remember them from when I was a girl. They've been painted grey to make them harder to spot by enemy U-boats. Not a ship has a light on. No bands are playing in golden ballrooms. There is only the steady hum of the ships and the breathing of men in hammocks and horses warming the walls with their bodies.

There are thousands of stars, the moon, and the single coal of a cigarette farther along the deck. It glows and dims on a face before flicking and falling to the silver waves.

Nice night.

CHARLIE   Yes, it is that. You on watch?

MARY   Just out for a walk.

CHARLIE   Is that you?

MARY   Of course it's me.

CHARLIE   Sergeant Flowerdew?

MARY   And in the dream I am that sergeant.

CHARLIE stands to attention.

CHARLIE   I'm sorry, sir, I thought you were someone else.

FLOWERS   Who'd you think I was? A girl in a nightie? As you were, man, and don't call me "sir," I work for a living.

CHARLIE relaxes.

You on watch?

CHARLIE   I was earlier, now I just can't sleep.

FLOWERS   What's the problem?

CHARLIE   Just thinking.

FLOWERS   What about?

CHARLIE   A girl, Sergeant.

FLOWERS   Well, if you've got to be up all night thinking, that's the best thing to be thinking about. Your first crossing, Edwards?

CHARLIE   Yes, Sergeant. This is the first time I've seen the ocean. I've heard good things about it, though.

FLOWERS   It's very calm, bright.

CHARLIE   Blue.

FLOWERS   It was like this when I crossed over to Canada.

CHARLIE   Where from?

FLOWERS   From England.

CHARLIE   You can see for miles. You'd think if they were out there . . . if the U-boats were out there, they could see us pretty good . . . if they were near here looking for us . . . they'd have some easy shooting.

FLOWERS   That's why we don't smoke on deck.

CHARLIE   . . .

FLOWERS   What's her name? Your girl's name?

CHARLIE   Mary, Sergeant.

FLOWERS   Mary Sergeant?

CHARLIE   No, Mary Chalmers. I don't know any Mary Sergeant.

FLOWERS   Charlie and Mary.

CHARLIE   Mary and Charlie. It doesn't really ring, does it?

FLOWERS   It rings just fine. Try going through your life with a name like Flowerdew. Gordon Muriel Flowerdew.

They used to call me Flowers when I was a boy . . . I just told you, so I imagine it'll be all over the regiment before we see land.

CHARLIE   I won't tell the regiment your nickname if you don't tell them I was afraid and couldn't sleep.

FLOWERS   Listen, Charlie, we're horse soldiers, this sailing isn't our kind of war. We'll be on land soon enough, back on our horses, where we belong. Then, if we get to France and the Germans before the war is over, they'll be in for it. Eh?

CHARLIE   Maybe we'll take 'em in a charge, then they'll be in for it.

FLOWERS   Can I give you some advice? From someone with some experience dreaming of someone far away?

        CHARLIE nods.

        Don't think about her too much. Or you won't be able to see anything else—you'll see her in everyone, everywhere you look.

CHARLIE   I already do.

FLOWERS   Get some sleep. We've got a big day ahead of us tomorrow, feeding horses and shovelling sh— There's a lot of shovelling, let me tell you.

CHARLIE   Yes, Sergeant.

> *CHARLIE takes up the loading of bags.*

FLOWERS   There's a lot of bags to be carried as well.

CHARLIE   Yes, Sergeant.

FLOWERS   Rest those shoulders.

CHARLIE   I'll try.

> *The ship fades to become the town at noon.* CHARLIE
> *loads the wagon while whistling "Rule Britannia!"*

MARY   I see him in town, loading his father's wagon. This is a
few days after we first met in the barn. I always notice
him first. I wonder whether he recognizes me. Then
he spies me too. We play a little game. It's called "We
don't see each other at all . . . Oh, hello!"

CHARLIE   Oh, hello!

MARY   Oh, hello! How is the work coming along?

CHARLIE   Fine.

MARY   I wasn't sure you recognized me.

CHARLIE   Oh, I did. I do. I mean, I did, how are you?

MARY   I'm, well . . . I'm me.

CHARLIE   I thought you were you . . . but I wasn't sure you'd recognize me.

MARY   Oh, I did . . . it just took a moment.

CHARLIE   Well, I'm dry and there's no storm, and I'm not shaking.

MARY   That's why. Charles "Charlie" Edwards. I remember. I'm in town . . . picking up the post.

CHARLIE   Looks like you've got it.

MARY   Mother is organizing the church tea this Saturday.

CHARLIE   Oh. Tea. Saturday?

MARY   You haven't heard? It is becoming quite the event. Mother loves to make a good impression.

CHARLIE   I don't go to very many teas.

MARY   I don't like them much either.

CHARLIE   Oh, I don't know if I like them or not. I'd have to go to know for sure. Are you going to be there?

MARY   Yes. I'll be there.

CHARLIE   Well, good.

MARY   Well, I guess I should be getting along.

CHARLIE   Um . . . the other day . . . during the storm, thank you for helping me to remember the poem. Maybe someday I'll be able to return the favour.

MARY   Oh, no trouble. Thank you, for the ride home. It was . . . it was, um . . . nice.

CHARLIE   It was nice, wasn't it? And sorry about the swearing.

MARY   Not at all. I swear all the time. Bloody hell, damn, damn, bloody hell, bollocks! Rest those shoulders.

That's how it happened in town. That's what we said. More or less. But we were happier to see each other than we both let on. We were playing a game. It's called "Try to not let your heart fly out of your mouth."

MARY looks through her mail as she walks. Behind her CHARLIE picks up a letter.

CHARLIE   Ah, Mary! You dropped something.

MARY   Wouldn't Mother be ecstatic? Thank you. Charlie?

CHARLIE   What is it?

MARY   It's from you.

CHARLIE   Really?

MARY   It's from England.

CHARLIE   From England?

MARY   When you go off to the war.

CHARLIE   Do I write you a lot when I'm away?

MARY   "Trooper Charlie Edwards."

CHARLIE   Well? Are you going to open it?

MARY   Can I?

CHARLIE   Open it. Open it.

          She opens the letter.

MARY   "Dear Mary." Look, that's me.

CHARLIE   Dear Mary.

MARY   "Well, you'll be glad to hear we've made the crossing without being sunk by U-boats."

CHARLIE   That's a relief.

MARY   "I've never been to the city but our camp in England seems like one. I've never seen so many people in one place at one time. And everyone, to the man, is eager to get over to the front and give it to the Germans.

I've seen some sights since I left home but the biggest thrill yet has been a meeting with King George."

CHARLIE That's right, Mary, I met the king of England—

MARY You fibber.

CHARLIE Well, me and the rest of the division.

MARY "There we were, more than twenty thousand of us, from British Columbia to Nova Scotia—infantry, cavalry, artillery—all Canadians, all formed up and ready. We practised for a week in the rain for his inspection. They tell us not to look around on parade but I couldn't help but steal a glance as he rode past."

CHARLIE He was much smaller than I thought he would be but his beard was exactly like in the painting in the schoolhouse. You're not going to believe this but just as he rode by . . . the sun came out and he looked right at me.

MARY He didn't.

CHARLIE He did too. Right at me.

MARY Then what happened?

CHARLIE Well, Flowers caught me staring—

MARY "Edwards, shut your trap, you're not catching flies."

CHARLIE   I don't think the king heard, though.

MARY   "His visit meant that some of us would get our chance to go to the front and it wasn't long before the infantry went over."

CHARLIE   They looked a proud bunch as they marched out to cross the channel. We formed up on parade and cheered them as they left.

MARY   "They went into the line at a place called . . . ?"

CHARLIE   Wipers, we call it.

MARY   Oh, Ypres.

CHARLIE   Yp-res.

MARY   "They had a tough go of it over there, as you may have read in the papers."

CHARLIE   Chlorine gas.

MARY   I did read it in the papers. No one ever used poison gas before. In the front trench our men looked over, as green clouds of fog rose up from the German lines and drifted along with the wind. It crept through the shell craters of No Man's Land, filling the hollows in the land but always teased by the wind, toward our lines. We heard it made you feel like you were drowning.

CHARLIE   But our boys were the only ones that held on, see?

CHARLIE takes the letter and reads on.

"They put up a tough fight and we're all proud of them."

MARY   The front trenches were filled like a mass grave. We read that in one day six thousand men were lost. Captured, wounded, dead. All those arms and voices.

CHARLIE   "They came to the cavalry and asked us to volunteer to go into the trenches dismounted—as infantry—to make up for the losses . . . "

MARY   They asked you to give up your horses?

CHARLIE   It's not something any good cavalryman wants to do but . . . the king looked right at me.

MARY   You said yes, didn't you?

CHARLIE   Every one of us. To the man.

MARY   I'm proud of you. Thank you for writing. I love your letters.

CHARLIE   There'll be more.

MARY   Promise.

S t e p h e n   M a s s i c o t t e

CHARLIE   Promise to write you all the time.

MARY   I'll be waiting. I should get home to help Mother with the preparations.

CHARLIE   I've got to get this home.

MARY   I'll see you, then?

CHARLIE   Maybe at the tea.

MARY   Maybe at the tea. If it's not raining.

CHARLIE   Maybe even then.

The Saturday afternoon tea.

MARY   And I'm at the tea, helping to make sure everything happens according to Mother's carefully orchestrated plans. Ladies and gentlemen talk in circles, according to plan. The pies are brought out, right on schedule, according to plan. I look all over the place for Charlie. And there he is. Oh, he looks like a proper gentleman. He even combed his hair.

CHARLIE   Good afternoon, Miss Chalmers.

MARY   Charles, good afternoon, sir. I didn't expect to see you here.

CHARLIE   Oh, but it's such a lovely day for a tea.

— 28 —

MARY   Well, don't leave us in suspense, what do you make of it?

CHARLIE   I've never really been to a tea. I mean I've had tea, but not been to a tea, so I couldn't really know for sure, until I'd actually been to a tea.

MARY   Well, now that you've actually been to one, how do you like it?

CHARLIE   It's nice, it's a tea, there's tea.

MARY   There is tea.

CHARLIE   To tell you the truth, I don't quite feel like I belong.

MARY   Then you are doing very well because you certainly look like you belong.

CHARLIE   Really?

MARY   Yes, you look like a regular tea-goer. A veteran of many teas.

CHARLIE   Charge!

MARY   Your hair looks nice.

CHARLIE   I . . . I comb it every day. I just combed it more today. I couldn't quite get all of it to stay down.

MARY   There is a bit standing up.

CHARLIE   Where?

MARY   Just a bit. At the back.

CHARLIE pats at his hair.

CHARLIE   Did I get it?

MARY   Still . . . it's . . .

CHARLIE   How's that?

MARY   Here, hold this, let me . . .

MARY attempts to straighten CHARLIE's hair.

CHARLIE   Uh . . . there's a lady waving at me. Hello! Boy, she's waving really hard. Maybe there's a fire. Something's got her pants in a knot, she's flapping around like an old hen.

MARY   Coming, Mother!

CHARLIE   Your mother? Hello, Mrs. Chalmers! Wonderful tea! . . . My first tea disaster.

MARY   I should really go and see what she wants before her arm flies off.

CHARLIE   Mm-hm.

MARY   I'll be right back. Don't go anywhere.

CHARLIE   I'll wait right here . . . Flapping around like an old hen?

> *Rain starts to fall.*

MARY   Then it starts to rain big wet spots on everyone's suits and dresses. And then a downpour. Ladies scream as everyone runs for cover. A dropped teacup shatters. A chair is overturned.

> *The sky darkens and there is a distant flash of lightning. CHARLIE looks straight up and waits.*

Charlie should find some shelter, but he just stands there looking up into the sheets of rain. Oh, I told him not to go anywhere.

CHARLIE   One-one thousand, two-one thousand, three-one thousand, four-one thous—

> *Thunder. Mixed into it is an artillery barrage and scattered machine-gun fire.*

MARY   That one was closer.

CHARLIE   Mary?

MARY   The storm worsens. Explodes. There are explosions. I see barbed wire.

CHARLIE   This isn't good. This is no good.

MARY   He is knee-deep in mud. He ducks his head into his shoulders as the thunder claps and shells burst. It's his first night at the front.

Lightning flash.

CHARLIE   One-one thousand, two-one thousand, three-one—

A thunder clap or a shell crash.

Oh my god. Oh my god, Mary. Shit.

MARY   I'm right here, Charlie.

CHARLIE   I swear too much.

Boom.

Bloody hell! Damn! Damn! Bloody hell! Bollocks!

Lightning.

MARY   A shell lands close.

Explosion. Thunder.

He is showered with mud and rain.

CHARLIE   Oh god, Mary, make it quiet! Make it quiet!

MARY   I can hear him breathing. His heart beating—

CHARLIE   "Cannon in front of them
Volley'd and thunder'd—"

BOTH   "Storm'd at with shot and shell—"

Lightning flashes and thunder claps, almost simultaneously.

CHARLIE   We have to get out of here! I have to get out of here!

MARY   Charlie, listen to me! "Boldly they rode and well, into the jaws of Death . . ." He doesn't listen or he cannot hear or . . . he was told to stay where he is. That was his last order.

CHARLIE panics and begins to abandon his position.

Charlie, don't! Just as he is about to run . . . just as he is about to disobey his orders . . . another shell comes in, up and behind Charlie, thumps deep into the soaked earth, explodes, and everything throws upward into the rain.

A whistle and a shell burst. CHARLIE is lifted up into the air with the erupting bank. It is suddenly very quiet.

Charlie, open your eyes, do you see? Look, just for an instant.

CHARLIE   . . .

MARY   For miles, the engraved zigzag of the trenches, the water-pocked No Man's Land reflecting like thousands of perfect mirrors, flights of machine-gun fire streaking quickly bright and out. There again, quickly bright and out. You can see it all from here. Charlie, open your eyes.

> *CHARLIE crashes back down to the ground.*

He sits in the shell hole, chest-deep in water, mud dripping off his nose and helmet. He sits still, trying to sense whether all of his body is there with him.

> *Lightning flashes.*

CHARLIE   "Into the mouth of Hell
Rode the six hundred."

Arms. Legs. Fingers. Toes. Ears. I can see. *(laughs)* That was a loud one.

> *A silence, then a far-off roll of thunder. CHARLIE drags himself up and back onto his feet. He waits under the tree at the tea for MARY.*

MARY   Are you all there?

CHARLIE   I think so. Yes. Are you?

MARY   Oh, yes, I'm all here.

A flicker of lightning.

CHARLIE   One-one thousand, two-one thousand, three-one thousand, four-one thousand, five—

Thunder rolls away.

It's going away.

MARY   They always do.

The rain is still lightly falling.

CHARLIE   Is everything all right with your mother?

MARY   Oh, yes. Just a little tea emergency.

CHARLIE   A tea emergency?

MARY   She wanted to know who you were. Whether you were "that dirty farm boy with the horse" who saw me home the other night.

CHARLIE   What did you tell her?

MARY   Does he look like a dirty farm boy?

CHARLIE   What did she say to that?

MARY   I brought an umbrella to rescue you.

He takes it just as the rain has faded away.

I'm sorry I wasn't more of a help to you out here all alone.

CHARLIE   No, I was just about to run off there when I remembered your advice. You saved the day.

MARY   "The Charge of the Light Brigade"?

CHARLIE   I'm glad I like it 'cause it's the only one I remember from school.

MARY   Why only that one?

CHARLIE   I love the charging-on-horseback parts, fast with your heart all pounding, with your voice just getting ready to shout all on its own. Kind of scary but good, you know? Like when I gave you a ride home.

MARY   Oh, it's always like that then.

CHARLIE   Always something like that, only that night there was something else that was ... different. That I never felt before.

MARY   Me too. What was it, do you think?

CHARLIE   I'm not sure. I think . . .

MARY   What?

CHARLIE   I think . . . maybe we could go riding again to . . .

MARY   I'll be coming back from town tomorrow afternoon. I've got some errands to run for Mother. The post. Perhaps we may bump into each other somewhere along the way?

CHARLIE   Maybe by the old barn?

MARY   By the turn in the road?

CHARLIE   Down from the bridge? Maybe.

MARY   These things do happen sometimes, somewhere along the way.

CHARLIE   They do.

MARY   Oh, Charlie?

He turns back to return her umbrella. She smooths the bit of hair that was standing up at the back of his head and the umbrella pops open. A steady roll of an artillery barrage can be heard farther off.

CHARLIE   "Dear Mary,

"There is not much sitting around allowed in the front line. There are holes and collapses everywhere from the rain and shelling. The water in the trench is a foot deep and the mud is deeper. But we do our best to keep our feet dry . . ."

MARY   How's the letter-writing?

CHARLIE   Good. All right. It could be better.

MARY   May I?

CHARLIE hands the letter over.

"Dear Mary." It starts well. Let's see . . . "Mud . . . mud . . . mud." Mud, Charlie?

CHARLIE   But I have to tell her something, Sergeant.

FLOWERS   What is it that you'd really like to tell her?

CHARLIE   Things.

FLOWERS   Keeping a brave face for the girl?

CHARLIE nods.

I should think that she'd like you to write about what's going on in here.

CHARLIE   But how do you write that?

FLOWERS With your pencil.

> *The artillery barrage intensifies.* CHARLIE *and*
> FLOWERS *look up to where shells whisper over them*
> *on their way to the enemy lines.*

The artillery's up again. Giving them a good pounding.

CHARLIE You can almost see them. What's it been? Twelve days' worth? Are you going over the top with the 5th Battalion's attack?

FLOWERS I see that you volunteered to go over with them.

CHARLIE They were bound to ask us to go over sooner or later.

FLOWERS Most of 1st and 3rd Troop are going over. That's plenty of volunteers.

CHARLIE Moss, Givan, and Cook are going.

FLOWERS In the last week the British haven't gained a mile and there have been more than twelve thousand casualties. One or two more isn't going to make a difference.

CHARLIE Everyone's got to do his share.

FLOWERS They need extra stretcher-bearers at the dressing station. What say you carry a stretcher this go-around?

> CHARLIE *shakes his head no.* FLOWERS *nods reluctantly.*

All right . . . don't stop for anything. Keep your spacing. Nice even lines. Don't bunch up. Listen for the officer's whistles and we go over.

CHARLIE   You're coming with us?

FLOWERS   Remember, fixed bayonet, ten in the magazine, one up the spout, but don't get to shooting until we get there. Keep it moving. We stop, we're done for.

CHARLIE   Yes, Sergeant.

FLOWERS   Yes, Sergeant. Good.

CHARLIE   Do you think there'll be anyone left alive when we get to them?

FLOWERS   Ah, don't give up hope. Our shelling is probably just keeping them ducking. Listen close for the commands, it's going to be noisy. Charlie?

BOTH   See you on the other side.

> *The artillery barrage continues its last waves. A watch begins ticking.*

CHARLIE   "Dear Mary,

"I'm writing this while we wait for the whistles. We're part of a big attack tonight. We're in the jump-off trench with the 5th Battalion, and we're all keen to give the Germans a good go."

MARY   Is that how it was?

CHARLIE   "They passed the rum ration around earlier and boy is my nose warm."

MARY   Keeping a brave face for the girl?

CHARLIE   Yes.

MARY   Tell me.

CHARLIE   It's hard to breathe. My mouth is dry, no spit. The trench is full of men packed in like sardines, all of us silent and swallowing. Close and damp. Our rifles are held tight, muzzle up, everyone leaning up against the trench wall. Eyes wide, listening, watching the nearest officer. He stares at his watch.

MARY   Wiping the mud from the face.

CHARLIE   A minute to two in the morning, the whistle is in his mouth.

MARY   His hand shakes.

The artillery stops and the watch ticking can clearly be heard.

CHARLIE   Then the whistles sound and the first line of the 5th Battalion climbs to the top of the trench wall. Right away, some of them pitch backward onto us. The German machine guns have started their raking. We catch bodies as they fall. Commands come. "First line, fix bayonets." At the top, they draw their knives and fix them to their rifles. Then the second whistle and the first line marches forward out of sight. We all wait and listen to the machine guns.

MARY   It doesn't stop? It continues?

CHARLIE   And then we hear the explosions of the German artillery. More follow. Bullets whistle over our heads and dig into the sandbags and dead bodies at the top.

MARY   What do you do?

CHARLIE   I look up to the stars but there's only sheets of rain lit by the flares. The whistles blow again and the 5th Battalion's second line clambers to the top of the trench. More of them pitch back onto us. We drag them down. "Second line, fix bayonets."

There is the ring of metal as the bayonets are fixed.

The whistles blow and the second line begins its march across No Man's Land. The machine guns continue to rake back and forth but there are rifle shots too. The first line must be shooting. Our boys are firing. Out there, they must have reached the Germans.

MARY   Then it was your turn, like the others?

CHARLIE   Yes. But we didn't walk. Right before we went over, Flowers passed an order down the line. Passed it man to man. "Forget about the spacing. Forget about the even lines, you hear me?"

MARY   What?

CHARLIE   "Run," he said. "You understand me? Run as fast as you can."

MARY   Run?

CHARLIE   And I passed it down, run all the way . . .

MARY   Run all the way . . . run all the way . . . run . . . run all the way . . .

CHARLIE   And we ran as we followed behind the 5th Battalion. We ran through the piles of the killed and wounded 5th Battalion. Strewn out there like old blankets. Heaped on top of each other. Beside each other. One behind the other. Screaming and grabbing at our legs as we ran by them. Over them. Tripping us up.

MARY   And all the while the machine guns kept firing and the shells kept falling?

CHARLIE   Yes, Mary. That's how it was. After the Battle of Festubert our wounded lay in No Man's Land until nightfall before we could go out to get them. Mary, back in our trenches, we had to spend the day listening to them . . . call to us.

MARY   All those arms and voices.

> *MARY waits by the side of the road. CHARLIE walks up to keep their date. He is leading his horse.*

CHARLIE   Hello, Mary.

MARY   Charlie, you made it. I'm so relieved.

CHARLIE   Did you think I wasn't going to?

MARY   I must confess I was a little worried.

CHARLIE   We practically ran the whole way. You've picked up the post.

MARY   And you were just, um . . . passing by . . .

CHARLIE   Well, since we're both here . . . shall we go for our ride?

MARY   Yes. Yes. Shall we?

CHARLIE   You can get on first.

MARY   Oh.

CHARLIE   Go on, mount up.

MARY   I'm afraid my equitation skills may be a bit rusty.

CHARLIE   We don't mind.

MARY   It's been a while.

CHARLIE   Up you go.

> *MARY goes to mount CHARLIE's horse.*

Left side, that's right. Reach up. Both hands like that. Just pull and throw your leg over. There you go. Good.

MARY   Are you coming up?

CHARLIE   I'll be up in a minute. You're all right.

> *MARY is mounted up on CHARLIE's horse. She sits very straight and still. Silence.*

You just going to sit there?

MARY   May I walk her a little?

CHARLIE   Well, you look silly just sitting there. Go ahead.

MARY   I've a confession to make. I've never . . . actually been on a horse by myself.

CHARLIE   What? A good English girl like you? Never studied equitation?

MARY   Equitation no, ballet and piano yes.

CHARLIE   Ballet, really? Can you dance?

MARY   First position?

CHARLIE   Can you play?

MARY   "God Save the King."

CHARLIE   Well, I guess we'll have to teach you to ride like a colonist.

MARY   What do I do first?

CHARLIE   First, we get you up in the saddle.

MARY   We've done that.

CHARLIE   Next we get you moving forward.

MARY   How do we do that?

CHARLIE   You just have to give her the hint.

> MARY *tries to get the horse moving. It stays still.* CHARLIE *looks on. She tries again. Nothing.* CHARLIE *waits. She thinks a moment and does the thing* CHARLIE *did to get the horse going. The horse walks forward.*

MARY   Oh, she just wants to go.

CHARLIE   It just has to be the right hint, that's all.

MARY   Turning right. There we go. Good girl.

CHARLIE   You've got it.

MARY   I've another confession to make.

CHARLIE   You're scared of horses.

MARY smiles.

You didn't seem so afraid when we rode home together.

MARY   Oh I was . . . but in a different way. I was frightened but you were there, with me, if you know what I mean?

CHARLIE   I think I do. Scary but good.

CHARLIE stops the horse.

MARY   Why are we stopping?

CHARLIE   I don't know.

MARY   I think you do.

He reaches up and touches her face. They kiss. Silence.

Another?

CHARLIE   If it's not too much trouble.

They kiss again.

BOTH   Scary but good.

MARY laughs.

CHARLIE   I like it when you laugh.

MARY   I like laughing at you . . . I mean, I like it when you make me laugh.

The horse steps forward a little.

Oh!

CHARLIE   Look, we've made her jealous.

MARY laughs and rides the mare around a little.

MARY   Well, she's just going to have to get used to it . . .

CHARLIE   Look at you. A natural.

MARY   I can't believe I'm doing this.

CHARLIE   Riding a horse?

MARY   Disobeying Mother.

CHARLIE   Is kissing a dirty old farm boy the worst thing you've
           ever done?

MARY   Best thing I've ever done.

CHARLIE   What would your mother think?

MARY   I'll do much worse.

           They kiss again.

           What's the worst thing you've ever done? Other than
           disobeying Mother?

CHARLIE   Other than that? I don't know. I'll tell you when I do it.

           What is it? What's that look?

MARY   Nothing.

CHARLIE   I can see it in your eyes. It's not good, is it?

MARY   No. No, I shouldn't have asked. Forget I mentioned it.

CHARLIE   Not now, I can't. You have to tell me. Please. Tell me.

MARY   If you really want to know, I'll tell you what it is.

CHARLIE   How do you know?

MARY   You told me in your letter today.

CHARLIE   I really want to know.

MARY   You finally saw a German soldier . . . Please, Charlie, we don't have to talk about this.

CHARLIE   Tell me.

MARY   On patrol, coming back, ten yards from your barbed wire, coming back through No Man's Land, you looked back before going in to sleep.

Night shades down around them.

CHARLIE   Do you see that? Right there, see?

Silence while they watch.

Right-there-right-there, Sergeant.

FLOWERS   . . .

CHARLIE   Do you see him?

FLOWERS   Who is it?

CHARLIE   A scout or . . . or a sniper?

FLOWERS   One of ours?

CHARLIE No . . . I don't know. I don't know. No.

FLOWERS . . .

CHARLIE What should we do?

FLOWERS We drop him. If he crosses that line, take him.

CHARLIE I see.

FLOWERS . . .

CHARLIE Go back. Come on, go back . . . Go back, go back,
please go back . . .

> *CHARLIE continues this mantra through MARY's next
> speech.*

MARY The sniper, the ghost, the German . . . person came
closer, from puddle to puddle, and you wished he'd go
back. You wished he would but he kept disappearing
and appearing, closer, like he was trying to catch up
to your patrol . . . until he crossed the line. You held
your breath. Then Flowers touched your shoulder and
your rifle made the sound . . .

> *CHARLIE's mantra stops.*

. . . of one quick stroke of an axe chopping wood.

> *Crack. Silence.*

CHARLIE There was a splash, too. A splash when he dropped into the water.

MARY Through your sights you saw this, while the spent casing was still hot in the smoking barrel, still pointed where he'd been standing. He bobbed up like he was floating in a lake in the summer, gazing up with the water ringing out around him. But then, slowly, he rolled over onto his front.

CHARLIE It's the worst thing I ever did.

> *Quiet.* MARY *holds her hand out to him. He takes it and mounts up behind her.*

MARY Oh, look, Charlie, how pretty a night it is. The stars are coming out. Look there . . .

CHARLIE It is pretty.

MARY Another fine lesson. Have I learned everything there is to learn?

CHARLIE You've got her jumping fences. I've never been able to make her do that.

MARY Really? No.

CHARLIE True. True. Cross my heart. On our first lesson after the tea, I would have never thought you'd be a better rider than me but here you are.

MARY   You flatterer.

CHARLIE   No flattery—you're an excellent student.

MARY   You're an excellent teacher.

           Pause.

           Charles "Charlie" Edwards?

CHARLIE   Mary Chalmers.

MARY   There is something I'd like to say to you.

CHARLIE   What?

MARY   Charlie, I . . . I . . .

CHARLIE   You what?

MARY   Thank you for the lessons.

CHARLIE   That's what you wanted to say?

MARY   Something like that, yes. Good night, Charlie.

           MARY has dismounted and CHARLIE moves off on his horse.

           Every time we get away together, it's over too soon. I tell him so many things but when we reach Mother's house there is always so much more to tell. It feels as though I hadn't told him a thing. But always the three words I want to say, I don't. Every night that he drops me off, I lie in bed rehearsing the words for the next time I see him. It is all our little secret, we think. But Mother knows. Nobody is so keen to get the post. And no one takes that long to do it.

CHARLIE sleeps.

FLOWERS   Wake up, Charlie, wake up.

CHARLIE   Are we going over again, Sergeant?

FLOWERS   No, Trooper, we're not going over. How are you doing?

CHARLIE   Fine.

FLOWERS   How are your feet? All right? Keeping them dry?

CHARLIE   Yeah.

FLOWERS   At least one of us is. Were you dreaming?

CHARLIE   Yeah, about the German that we shot on patrol.

FLOWERS   Don't think so much. Don't let yourself think so much.

CHARLIE   I wasn't thinking. That's the trouble. I was dreaming.

FLOWERS   Well, dream about this, then. I've got news. We're relieved. So pack up, fifteen minutes.

CHARLIE   Are we getting our horses back?

FLOWERS   It's not that news. We get to go out, rest, clean up for a couple of weeks, then we're back in the line.

CHARLIE   Where?

FLOWERS   Here. Or somewhere else. I don't know.

CHARLIE   In the line, though?

FLOWERS   In the line. Where else?

> *CHARLIE walks away. The sky gleams through the slats and roof holes of the barn. MARY sits and reads.*

MARY   "Down she came and found a boat
Beneath a willow left afloat,
And round about the prow she wrote
The Lady of Shalott."

CHARLIE   Mary.

MARY   Charlie, there you are.

CHARLIE   You're all alone.

MARY   Just me and a little poetry. "The Lady of Shalott."

CHARLIE   What's it about?

MARY   A maiden who falls in love with a knight.

CHARLIE   Sounds nice.

MARY   He can't love her so she dies of heartbreak floating down the river.

CHARLIE   Ow. Really? That's sad. Does she drown or go over the falls or something?

MARY   No, she dies of heartbreak for him.

CHARLIE   She doesn't fall in the river?

MARY   Her unfulfilled love for him is enough to make her die of heartbreak. That's the way it's done. Listen.

"For ere she reach'd upon the tide
The first house by the water-side,
Singing in her song she died,
The Lady of Shalott."

CHARLIE   I see.

MARY   How did you know I was here?

CHARLIE   Where else would I find you?

MARY   Did you go by my house?

CHARLIE   I rode past. Said hello to Mother.

MARY   You didn't!

CHARLIE   I rode up and asked if you were around.

MARY   What did she say?

CHARLIE   She said you were out with a boy . . .

MARY   My mother said that? Wonderful!

CHARLIE   Oh, she was nice.

MARY   She didn't say anything else to you?

CHARLIE   No, nothing else.

MARY   Nothing at all? She was on her best behaviour, then. She's got her mind set on the kind of gentleman that I should marry.

CHARLIE   Not one of the colonists?

MARY   Not dirty farm-boy colonists, anyway. Well, Charlie, you've found me out. I'm secretly in love with Alfred Lord Tennyson. It's been quite torrid out here in the barn, even if he isn't Lord Byron.

CHARLIE   I was thinking, Mary . . . that maybe I'm . . . not . . . the right sort of . . .

MARY   On the train trip here I saw them every so often . . . old sway-backed barns with an empty-windowed farmhouse. I wonder who lived here. I wonder about their lives, what happened to them, do you know what I mean?

CHARLIE   Maybe they went somewhere new? Somewhere happier where they could start over?

MARY   Or perhaps they lived here in love and squalor. And they raised many happy children together till one day they died old and grey in each other's arms. I bet if we look, we'll find their resting place side by side under that big tree out there.

CHARLIE   That's not very romantic.

MARY   Oh, yes it is.

CHARLIE   Now, it's just us here.

MARY   Just us?

CHARLIE   I can't stay today, Mary. Work has been piling up a bit with my father.

MARY   Stay with me.

CHARLIE   I have to go.

MARY   Charlie, wait.

But Charlie doesn't wait. He leaves because of Mother. He leaves because he loves me. I don't know why he leaves. I see him working on his father's farm. I see him from the road when I pass. He works very hard. He doesn't look up. He thinks work will help him forget. But he's wrong.

CHARLIE works at the sandbags again.

Stop a minute and listen to me.

CHARLIE   These sandbags need a little work here, Sergeant.

FLOWERS   I was talking to the quartermaster . . . Charlie!

CHARLIE keeps working.

Put the bag down, Trooper!

CHARLIE   Sergeant.

FLOWERS   I want to talk to you.

CHARLIE   I was listening.

FLOWERS   I know. Just sit down for a minute. How are you doing? Cold not getting to you? Hey, Charlie, keeping warm?

CHARLIE   I'm fine.

FLOWERS   Listen, I was looking at the records and it looks like
            you've been out in No Man's Land every night this
            week. And I hear you volunteered to go out on patrol
            again tonight?

CHARLIE   Everyone's got to do his share.

FLOWERS   Yes, his share, not everyone else's. You'll tire yourself
            out. You'll get knocked on some stupid patrol around
            in the mud—or even worse you'll get me knocked. Is
            there something you want to tell me?

CHARLIE   No.

FLOWERS   Nothing at all?

CHARLIE   No. Nothing.

FLOWERS   You're not going out tonight. No patrols for you until
            I say so.

CHARLIE   But, Sergeant—

FLOWERS   Save yourself. You don't want to use yourself up before
            your big charge . . . before you get back to Mary, do
            you? All right then, it's settled, you're staying in
            tonight. It's settled, right? "Yes, Sergeant" is the answer
            to that question.

CHARLIE   Yes, Sergeant.

Night falls and, with it, big glowing snowflakes.

MARY   I see the nights and patrols pass in No Man's Land and Charlie sits out. I see the nightly ambushes. I see the grenades tossed over at each other. I see them drag back the dead. Flowers keeps him out for as long as he can but the night comes when Charlie must take his turn.

> *MARY stands above him as CHARLIE crawls by on patrol.*

He crawls in the snow. He is nearly by me and he looks up and I see him.

CHARLIE   An angel. There are angels on the moon.

MARY   He just looks at me and I look at him. Then there is shooting. They fire into the dark, and somewhere out in the dark there are voices and arms that fire back.

> *A sudden burst of rifle fire. CHARLIE is hit. The volley continues and sporadically lessens to occasional popping.*

Charlie's blood melts the snow under him. The men of the patrol crowd in, drag him up, and huddle him back to their line. I can only watch as they drag him farther and farther away through the snow. And as they do, he looks back down a long red streak to see whether I am still standing here, waiting.

Soon, I am the only one left out here in a place that looks like the moon. I am alone on the moon and Charlie is bleeding somewhere far away. I can do nothing about it. I never can do anything about it. And just like it always does, war begins, and I cannot do anything about it.

CHARLIE approaches MARY.

I see that summer night of my birthday, perfectly warm, after the hot day. The boys and men talk with my father about the Kaiser's troops on Belgian soil, whether they will withdraw, whether it will lead to war. Great Britain made Germany an ultimatum. I hear them speculate but it doesn't seem to mean anything to me. Music plays but I don't move to a note of it.

There's the punch I don't drink. I see the lights and streamers that wreath the portrait of the king. He looks quite concerned about Charlie's absence.

CHARLIE   Happy birthday, Mary.

MARY   Charles "Charlie" Edwards.

CHARLIE   Do you think they'll throw me out?

MARY   Maybe I should let them.

CHARLIE   I didn't bring a present.

MARY   Yes, you did. Dance with me.

CHARLIE   Should we call the doctor first?

MARY   For Mother?

CHARLIE   For your poor wee toes.

MARY   You could kiss them better.

CHARLIE   My proper English girl.

MARY   Do you know what you say when a girl asks you to kiss her toes?

CHARLIE   No, what?

MARY   You say, "Yes, ma'am."

He holds his hands out for her and they dance.

I knew you wouldn't stay away. I knew you couldn't.

CHARLIE   I thought that maybe . . . you might be able to . . . you know . . . wake up and find someone a bit better suited for you.

MARY   A bit better suited for me? Like who?

CHARLIE   Someone who . . . someone who is . . .

MARY What? Richer? Smarter?

CHARLIE No.

MARY For goodness' sake, she may act like it but Mother is not Queen Victoria.

CHARLIE Well, I learned something staying away.

MARY Oh, and what did you learn?

CHARLIE I learned that I am a stupid, stupid boy.

MARY Ha! It's you, Charlie, only you.

CHARLIE I want this to last forever.

MARY Me too.

> *As they dance MARY sees the top of a letter in CHARLIE's shirt pocket.*

Is that a letter for me? I thought you said you didn't bring a present?

CHARLIE Oh, that'll keep.

MARY Charlie. What do you have to say?

CHARLIE Just dance with me.

She takes the letter from CHARLIE's shirt pocket. She opens it and reads.

MARY   "Dear Mary,

"I have been wounded."

Oh, my god. Where?

CHARLIE looks with surprise to his wound.

CHARLIE   In the east of France.

MARY   Charlie!

CHARLIE   Here.

He shows her the wound.

MARY   Oh, my poor Charlie!

CHARLIE   It'll be all right in the end, Mary. We will be happy.

MARY   Of course we will.

CHARLIE   Everything will be all right in the end.

MARY   Of course, everything will be all right, Charlie.

She pulls his shirt aside to see the spot where the bullet entered. She gently touches it with the tip of her finger.

CHARLIE   Ow.

FLOWERS   Trooper, steady up, man!

> *CHARLIE's wound has healed. They both look at its progress.*

Ah, is that what the big fuss was about? You might be able to impress your girl with that . . . What, did they use two whole inches of thread on it?

CHARLIE   They did a pretty good job, Sergeant.

FLOWERS   Wrong rank. You owe me a beer for that one.

CHARLIE   Oh, my god, you've been promoted. No more working for a living?

FLOWERS   That's right, Trooper, it's Lieutenant Flowers from now on.

CHARLIE   An officer?

FLOWERS   Who'd have thought?

CHARLIE   Did they give you 1st Troop?

FLOWERS   No.

CHARLIE   Aw, 2nd?

FLOWERS No.

CHARLIE What? Don't tell me Supply?

FLOWERS The squadron.

CHARLIE C Squadron Commander! That's wonderful.

FLOWERS Scary but good.

CHARLIE When did this happen?

FLOWERS You've been out for a while now. They didn't just end the war because Charlie couldn't be in it.

CHARLIE Well, then . . .

FLOWERS Shall we get it over with?

CHARLIE Congratulations, sir!

They salute and shake hands.

FLOWERS Well, I guess you're ready to come back to us, unless you've got a hangnail you want them to look at.

CHARLIE They said I could go yesterday.

FLOWERS Then I've got a surprise for you.

CHARLIE stops in his tracks. He's seen their horses.

CHARLIE   We've got our horses back.

FLOWERS   No more infantry duty for us. We're in reserve, waiting
           for a breakthrough. But it's been pretty quiet up front.

CHARLIE   Really? I still hear some shelling.

FLOWERS   Ah, the Germans, they just drop three or four every
           now and then, in case they might get lucky. I think it
           means the fight is out of them, we've got them on the
           run. Here, I picked this one out for you.

CHARLIE   Hello there.

           CHARLIE inspects his horse.

FLOWERS   They're as healthy as you are. Healthier maybe. They've
           had more exercise.

CHARLIE   It's all the hospital food.

           CHARLIE touches and pats her.

           We going to save the day, me and you? Sure, we can.
           Sure, we will.

FLOWERS   Are you two going to stand around necking all day?
           Or are we going to see whether you still know how to
           ride after all this time crawling around in the mud?

CHARLIE   That sounds like a challenge to me.

CHARLIE mounts up.

FLOWERS   Take it however you like.

> *CHARLIE and FLOWERS line themselves up on their horses and when they are ready, they begin the race.*

CHARLIE   Say when.

MARY   When!

We race out of the hospital yard and out into the sunny countryside. We fly past the slow ambulance trucks on the dirt roads. The hedgerows and fields and trees shade us for flickering moments and we flash again into the afternoon brightness. The trees come up fast and, through their leaves, the sky flashes by like water on a pond. He gets smaller as I watch him from higher and higher.

I am his air and wind. I am his swirling sky looking down above him. Up here it's quiet when I am still and when I listen closely, I can hear his horse's hooves and the sound of his laughing voice.

CHARLIE   Hold on, we'll be home soon!

MARY   And as he disappears and the sun begins to set, I can smell rain coming.

MARY takes in the smell of the rain. CHARLIE approaches very gently. He stops and lets her breathe a few more times before interrupting. The sky flickers with far-off lightning.

CHARLIE   Did you hear the news?

MARY   Yes, Charlie. Yes, I did. Who hasn't?

CHARLIE   "Great Britain declared war on Germany . . ."

MARY   " . . . and Canada pledges her support by offering troops." That's what the headlines say. What did they really expect to happen? How did you get past Mother?

CHARLIE   She let me in, said you were reading in here.

MARY   Oh, she invited you in, did she? She's changed her opinion of farm boys and colonists all of a sudden.

CHARLIE   I think maybe she liked me after all.

MARY   I think she likes you more now that you're going to fight for the British Empire.

CHARLIE   How do you know I'm going?

MARY   Isn't everybody? That's all they're talking about in town. All the men in my father's office are signing up together.

CHARLIE   Everyone must do his share.

MARY   Charlie.

CHARLIE   I went to militia camp last summer with my cousin.

MARY   So?

CHARLIE   I can shoot.

MARY   So what? That's what they're all saying at my father's office, but they're all just clerks. They file papers and fill their pens and now they think they're soldiers?

CHARLIE   I can ride.

MARY   I know you can. But you don't have to.

CHARLIE   I want to join the cavalry. I've always wanted to. Like in "The Charge of the Light Brigade."

MARY   Like in "The Charge of the Light Brigade"? Do you listen to yourself when you speak it? "Not tho' the soldier knew someone had blunder'd"? "Into the jaws of Death"? "Into the mouth of Hell"?

CHARLIE   But "When can their glory fade?" "Honour the charge they made!"

MARY   That's poetry, Charlie, not real life.

CHARLIE They need men who can ride. I can ride. I love to ride. You know what it's like, Mary. The wind and the sky? Your heart beating faster, louder than the hooves. You remember?

MARY I just thought . . .

CHARLIE What? Tell me.

MARY I thought that it was us. I thought it was us, the wind and the sky, faster and louder than the hooves. If you don't come home, I'll die of heartbreak.

CHARLIE That's poetry, Mary, not real life.

She turns away. Silence.

I have to go.

MARY Then go.

CHARLIE I want to ask you . . . if you'll meet me in the barn tonight.

MARY For what?

Pause.

Why?

CHARLIE There's something I want to ask you.

MARY   No, I won't. Not if you're going to go.

CHARLIE   But, Mary—

MARY   If you are going to war, then go. I don't care. I won't stop you.

CHARLIE   Please, meet me in the barn.

MARY   I said go away!

Pause.

GO!

CHARLIE walks away.

I see Charlie after he left my house. He walks his horse down the road through the puddles left by the dark rain heading far away east. I always wish right then for him to come back. For him to turn around and come back to me and he almost does. He almost turns back, but then he remembers I told him to go and he slowly follows after the flickering lightning at the edge of the sky.

The sky flickers with lightning far off.

CHARLIE   Sir? What's the news?

FLOWERS   Charlie, I was daydreaming for a second there.

FLOWERS looks off at the horizon.

CHARLIE   Are we moving out?

FLOWERS   Yes, Charlie. Ten minutes. Maybe.

CHARLIE   Do you know what's up?

FLOWERS   The enemy has been saving it up for one last offensive. They hit the French hard and punched a hundred-mile hole in the line.

CHARLIE   A hundred-mile hole in the line?

FLOWERS   They're just holding now until they bring up reinforcements, then they're going to gather steam in a straight line headed for Paris.

CHARLIE   Our brigade's got the job to fill in the hole?

FLOWERS   We of the Canadian cavalry are to hold as long as we can until the infantry can reform defences behind us.

CHARLIE   If we don't?

FLOWERS   Then they're going to roll right into Paris. And that'll be it. From the sounds of it, there's a lot of them.

CHARLIE   Across the river there?

FLOWERS   They're thick in the woods, the Bois de Moreuil, it's called. It's us, and the rest of the brigade. We're going to attack it.

CHARLIE   For sure?

FLOWERS   Sounds like it. As sure as it ever gets.

CHARLIE   Mounted? Maybe we'll take 'em in a charge, just like we said?

FLOWERS   Maybe, Charlie. But orders are to ride up and fight our way through the woods on foot.

CHARLIE   It's better than the trenches.

FLOWERS   It is that. How's everyone?

CHARLIE   Standing to.

FLOWERS   Charlie?

CHARLIE   Yes, sir?

FLOWERS   . . .

CHARLIE   You all right? What is it?

FLOWERS smiles.

FLOWERS   Nothing. You ready? Mount up.

CHARLIE   We cross the bridge. Our biplanes take passes at the wood, dropping bombs down into the branches. By the time we're over, the other cavalry squadrons are already fighting dismounted into the trees. We ride forward to dismount and join in when the general rides up and Flowers halts us.

MARY   A change of plans?

CHARLIE   Flowers turns to us. "Listen up, boys. We don't attack here with the others. The general thinks we can work in through the back of the wood and meet up with our boys in the middle. Surround them. We're going for a ride."

MARY   That's good news. It's going well.

CHARLIE   We just have to go for a ride. With any luck we'll catch them retreating. We're all excited and the horses can smell it. We head off. It's like riding in the fields back home. Pretty and easy. The bounce in the saddle, the spring in my legs, the sound of our harnesses, like sleigh bells.

We round the back of Moreuil Wood, out in the open. Fields of blue and green, waves like the ocean. And men in the waves. Flowers stands up tall in the saddle to see. Enemy troops set in two lines, fixed bayonets, a cannon. Machine guns on the flanks. An ambush.

MARY   Oh, god, they're waiting for you.

CHARLIE   They open fire. There are hits among us. My mare's
           ears flick. The cannon fires and dirt sprays up, a horse
           screams, things fly through the air. We can't turn back.
           Flowers rings out his sabre.

MARY   It's a charge, Charlie, it's a charge!

CHARLIE   We flash all our sabres bare and our horses race to
           catch up with him. The long blades of grass blend
           together and blur with speed. I crouch low with my
           head beside hers. She breathes.

MARY   Hish-ah, hish-ah, hish-ah.

CHARLIE   Flowers is flying, his sabre rolling over and over in
           forward circles, waving the charge on. He is shouting.
           I can hear it through my stirrups into my spurs and
           boots. I am catching up to you, Flowerdew!

BOTH   CHARGE! CHARGE! CHARGE!

           CHARLIE is giddy with excitement.

CHARLIE   His foot loses a stirrup. His horse twists and tumbles.
           Flowers is down. We leap over them. We are charging,
           Mary. I am charging faster than anyone ever.

           MARY stands with her eyes closed.

MARY   One-one thousand, two-one thousand, thr—

CHARLIE   Before I plunge into the smoke, a bird flashes across our path. His wings flicker three times and he pushes himself, flicker three times and we're gone by him. My sabre pulls my shoulder as it pierces a man there. Right through the line we break and we charge the kneeling second line.

MARY   One-one thousand, two-one—

CHARLIE   One of them raises his rifle to shield himself. I club at his head. My sabre falls in once, twice, three times. She leaps forward again, panicked, making for the open fields. She wants to keep running until her heart bursts. I fight to rein her in, to bring her around to attack again and then . . . I see what's behind me.

Beyond the man I just struck down there's the confusion we crashed into. Germans and Canadians—some still shooting, some crawling behind the cover of dead horses. A trooper, I don't know who, carrying another like in a three-legged race. Then they both fall. Another trying to remount his horse with one arm dripping red beside him. His foot keeps slipping. And amongst all that, one horse grazing, calmly picking at the grass as if he'd spent his whole life chewing in an old farmer's field.

MARY   RUN, CHARLIE, RUN! PLEASE!

CHARLIE   And then I wake, kick her to a gallop, and we race for the wood. I dismount and fire at the cannon, at the lines of Germans, at the machine guns on their flanks.

When they're dead, I fire at the men retreating. I fire. I reload. I fire. I reload. I fire. I reload. I fire. I sight a man careful. I fire. I do not get tired of it.

> *The sound of battle fades. Then a single shot rings out. When it doesn't seem like there will be any more, another shot follows. CHARLIE sits and breathes in near exhaustion. MARY quietly approaches.*

MARY   Charlie, are you all right?

CHARLIE   I twisted my shoulder a little.

MARY   Not a scratch. I saw you.

CHARLIE   You did?

MARY   You did it. You got your charge.

CHARLIE   Hold still, Flowers, the stretcher-bearers will be here in a minute.

> *FLOWERS staggers from his wounds. CHARLIE catches him and eases him to the ground.*

FLOWERS   You're all right?

CHARLIE   My mare's got a nicked hoof . . . Sir, hold still, don't move.

FLOWERS   Couple of good ones through the legs.

CHARLIE   They're not that bad.

FLOWERS   Bad enough, I think . . . 'twill serve.

CHARLIE   No, sir, no, sir. You won a ticket home.

FLOWERS   I'll be making the crossing without you.

CHARLIE   You'll . . . you'll be up in no time.

There is another shot.

FLOWERS   Is there anyone else?

CHARLIE   There are a lot left. They're coming in, lots wounded. Looks like you'll have plenty of company in hospital.

Another shot.

FLOWERS   What's that shooting?

CHARLIE   That's . . . that's the horses, sir.

FLOWERS   Are there a lot of them hurt?

CHARLIE   Yes, sir, there are a lot of them hurt. They're putting them down. We're back to the mud. I heard someone firing his pistol after you went down. Was that you?

FLOWERS   Took a few shots at that cannon.

CHARLIE   Someone said they'll put you up for a VC for sure.

FLOWERS doesn't hear. He is fading quickly.

FLOWERS   . . . Charlie?

CHARLIE   Yeah.

FLOWERS   I saw you. From where we fell. I was pinned under but I could still see. You were there first. You charged. You got to charge.

CHARLIE   I thought everyone was right behind me.

FLOWERS   You went through both lines.

CHARLIE   I didn't know I was the only one. I thought everyone was right behind me but I was really just by myself. The charge, it wasn't . . . poetry.

One last shot.

FLOWERS   Charlie, listen to me, are there two lines of Germans there now?

CHARLIE   No. Not anymore.

FLOWERS   Then we did our share. That will have to be enough . . . I told you you'd see her everywhere you looked.

CHARLIE   She's in everything.

FLOWERS fades and CHARLIE turns away.

"Dearest Mary,

"There is no more Flowers.

"I want to meet you in our barn. I never want to leave you again. I miss you more than anything. I miss you so much. I want to be home with you and never leave you again. I will love you and you will be happy. I promise you that. In the end you will be happy.

"Love . . ."

CHARLIE waits for MARY in the barn.

MARY   And this is how it ends. I never went to see him, but in this dream I do. We're in the barn. Charlie is. He is waiting for me. Nervous and shy, waiting to sail away on the grey ship full of horses.

The night that I never came to say goodbye. It's the night he waited to ask me and he left the next morning. But in this dream I go to see him. I go to stop him. I go to tell him.

CHARLIE   Mary? I'm glad you came.

MARY   You didn't think I would, did you?

CHARLIE   I wasn't too sure.

MARY   So, you're going?

CHARLIE   I am. I am. I have to.

MARY   I know.

CHARLIE   I shouldn't have come by and told you like that.

MARY   I shouldn't have told you to go away the way I did.

CHARLIE   It's all right, I'd have given me the boot too. All I can say is, whether or not you write to me, your mailbox will be full all the time. I promise. I'll write you non-stop, you'll see. I'm going to miss you a lot, Mary, because . . . well, because I . . . Well, maybe you won't miss me but I'll miss you.

MARY   Yes, I will. Yes, I do. I miss you very badly. Every minute.

CHARLIE   Maybe it won't be too long and then—

MARY   Charlie—

CHARLIE   Then we can be married.

MARY   Yes, that would be wonderful.

CHARLIE   It'll be sunny. You'll be in one of those pretty white dresses and we can have our portrait taken and we can have children. We'll have children, not right away. Two girls and one boy—

MARY   Two boys and one girl.

CHARLIE   And we'll have horses for all the little colonists.

MARY   Charlie, listen, for a minute, please. It sounds lovely but . . . just listen. I went to get the post today.

CHARLIE   Did I write?

MARY   There wasn't anything there.

CHARLIE   Oh. Well, I bet there will be something tomorrow. Or the day after. You know how slow the mail is.

MARY   There won't be any more letters.

CHARLIE   Sure, there will. I write you all the time. I just promised.

MARY   The last one that arrived was the one after the charge at Moreuil Wood. The one where you told me you wanted to come home. You said, "I want to come home now. I want to meet you in our barn. I never want to leave you again."

Something is slowly dawning on CHARLIE.

CHARLIE   What is it, Mary? What happened?

MARY   I met your father today in town.

CHARLIE   How's he doing? I miss him already.

MARY   He misses you too. The farm is well. There are two new mares. He said that he'd gotten a message. News.

CHARLIE   Did Flowers get his medal?

MARY   Yes.

CHARLIE   Lieutenant Gordon Muriel Flowerdew, Victoria Cross.

MARY   It's hard to forget a name like that. No, it was a telegram. You and the Canadian Cavalry Division stopped the German advance. Some say you saved the war.

CHARLIE   That's good, isn't it?

MARY   It is good, I suppose. I'm trying. I'm trying. You were in a field. You and all of your tents. A German plane flew by at night and strafed the regiment while you were camped.

CHARLIE   Was anyone hurt?

She shakes her head.

How about the horses?

MARY No, but they were scattered . . . and you had to—all of you—had to go and find them where they'd run off to. And it took all night to find the horses and . . . the German artillery was shelling places where there might be regiments camped out. They just dropped three or four every now and then, in case they might get . . . in case they might happen to drop some shells on anyone who might happen to be out there. Out there looking for their horses.

CHARLIE They do that all the time. It's a sign that we've got them on the run, that they're getting desperate. The fight is out of them.

MARY But, Charlie, I have to tell you . . . I have to tell you. You've come and found her in a field. She wakes up from her dream and stands up. You touch her and step by her neck and shoulder. You calm her. The sun is rising. You're happy. She's happy. She is unhurt and you can bring her back home. I dream it all the time.

CHARLIE That's when they shelled the field?

MARY I swear you hear them. You look up at the sky. The two of you don't move and I always wonder why. You just stand beside her looking up at the sky.

CHARLIE We're going to count the thousands from the flash to the rumble.

MARY Yes.

CHARLIE   Before they land . . . before I . . . before I die . . . do I say anything?

MARY   Yes. Something. I can't make it out. I'm sorry.

CHARLIE   I guess we won't be getting married. I guess we don't.

MARY   I'm sorry.

CHARLIE   I'm sorry, too.

MARY holds CHARLIE's face in her hands.

MARY   I nearly die of heartache. I swear, for months I can't move. For months I float down the river with my name on the prow.

CHARLIE   But you get better, though.

MARY   I do.

CHARLIE   You don't die.

MARY   I live.

CHARLIE   You love someone good. Please tell me you marry someone good?

MARY   Not yet. Tomorrow.

CHARLIE   Just love him as well as you can and be happy. Please.

MARY   I'm sorry, Charlie. I'm sorry I never came to see you in the barn.

CHARLIE   You did tonight.

MARY   I'm sorry I never stopped you from going.

CHARLIE   You did tonight.

MARY   I'm so sorry. It's the worst thing I ever did. And I can't forget you.

CHARLIE   Don't forget. Just let go.

MARY   I'm trying to. It's just you're in everything. All the time.

CHARLIE   Let me be in everything. Just a little less maybe.

MARY   Will you always be there?

CHARLIE   Yes, Mary, always. Only a little less. I've got to go now.

A far-off roll of thunder sounds. MARY and CHARLIE look to it.

MARY   No, don't go. Don't go. Please, stay with me.

CHARLIE   I can't stay. I have to go now and it's time for you to wake up.

MARY   I can't.

CHARLIE   Yes, you can.

MARY   Please, don't go. Kiss me, please.

> *They kiss. They hold on very tightly.*

CHARLIE   I love you.

MARY   I love you so much.

CHARLIE   You . . . you are the best thing, the very best thing. I'll see you someday.

MARY   I hope so. I do hope so.

> *CHARLIE slowly lets go of MARY.*

There's a thunderstorm coming.

CHARLIE   I don't mind getting a little wet.

MARY   What are you going to do?

CHARLIE   I don't know. I think . . . I think I'll just go and . . . I think I'll just go for a ride . . . I'll just go out for a little ride in the fields. Just enjoy the rain for a while.

> *MARY's composure begins to slip.*

Don't worry, it'll be over by the time you wake up. Mary's wedding will be sunny. In a little while, you are going to wake up and I will have been lying under the grass for nearly two years now. You are going to wake up and you will never have this dream again. And when you wake up, this is what I see:

I see you in a white dress at the church. I see your mother and friends helping you with your hair and yellow flowers. And you are beautiful. I can see tears on your face as you walk down the aisle with all your friends and family smiling for you. People think you are crying because of all the excitement. You walk slowly with your face looking at the floor. You try very hard to take every step. And just before you get up to the front, your eyes slowly rise and you see the face of the good man you are going to marry. And slowly, like a sunrise, you smile and your heart is like the clear blue sky. You smile, Mary.

And outside a soft wind blows and in that wind there is the very faint sound of a horse riding in the fields.

Just barely it's there, faint in the summer wind.

MARY   How do you know?

CHARLIE Because I'm in it.

> *The sound of a light breeze can be heard.* CHARLIE *stands off in the deep blue, but is not gone.*

MARY   And that's the end of the dream. It begins at the end and ends at the beginning. Like before, Charlie rides away thinking of me, only this time he doesn't go away. This time there is no more war. This time he rides off into the fields.

When I awake, the day, my dress, and my husband are waiting. It's a July wedding on a Saturday morning in nineteen hundred and twenty. I still think of him.

I see him on horses. I see him running with them, in dreams, in waking, in forests, in evenings, and in mornings. I hear him laughing and riding swiftly through fields. I hear him in church bells. I see white dresses, flowers, and little babies and Charlie is there in all of it. Only now a little less. Only now a little bit less. And that will be enough. Goodbye, Charlie.

CHARLIE   Goodbye, Mary. Do you want to know what I say before the shells land?

MARY   Yes, please.

CHARLIE   Wake up, Mary. Wake up.

> *They smile at each other from a distance. Then, as they leave separately, the wind rises gently and the church bells ring. Behind that, farther off as the sun rises, the sound of a single horse riding away into the distance.*
>
> *All of this is very pretty.*
>
> *End.*

AFTERWORD

For a history buff, armchair general, and reader of biographies like myself, the past is often more real than my present. It's like my own personal time machine. I leap through decades, from century to century, and back again, by switching chapters. For smaller jumps, I flip pages. Grabbing another book from the shelf takes me back millennia and sits me beside Socrates in a shady spot in Athens. My faves—Lawrence of Arabia, Hemingway, Brando—are resurrected for a few bucks whenever I fish out another biography at a used bookstore. Though I claim it's to make me good at trivia, I really do it to escape the mortality of the present, to find some existential freedom with a library card.

The trouble is, like most escapism, it doesn't last, and sooner or later it collapses spectacularly. My time machine falls apart: I'm actually powerless to stop the doomed attack, foil the assassination, or nudge it so that the Führer's mother never meets his father. Byron dies from a stupid cold that any one of us could have cured—*Begone with that bloodletting, fetch me chicken broth and all the citrus you can find!* The now comes back and I realize that the past does not exist, not here or anywhere. I don't have a time machine, just an overactive imagination. I could sooner swim the Atlantic than have that dinner with six historical figures of my choice. I may as well put away my calligraphy kit—no need for those invites and place cards; my guests don't exist and I, their host, am stranded here, now.

Old buildings or houses have assured me that the past was, at one time, real. With no historical importance other than their having survived, over the years, the "acts of god"—flood, fire, etc.— they're my favourites as I pass by on the bus. I've even managed to live in a few for a while. But I could never stop wondering which bathroom fixtures or walls were added in later renos. There must have been a time when the radiators were not thick with paint drippings and didn't clang as much. When the edge of the steps was not yet worn into a stone sag. It's sad when these buildings get knocked down to make way for some condo-bank-drugstore combo. But what can I—or anyone else—do about it? There are rats in the walls, lead in the pipes, and who wants to take cold, weak showers with sudden scalding blasts? And slim chance of heritage preservation; the people that wore down the stairs are not prize-winning non-fiction bestseller material. Their kids may have been conceived in those rooms, but then, that's nothing all that special. Again, history leaves, and me, I'm left to wear down some stairs.

I lean in close to the display glass in museums. I try out stories: *Was that comb handed down from mother to daughter near the banks of the Nile?* I think, *Was it a cherished comb, or more like my current toothbrush? What was the name of the Mesopotamian boy charging his toy horseman about the kitchen? Was that thimble loaned, but never returned because the lender couldn't remember (for the life of them) who they'd loaned it to?* The display cards—Egyptian Comb, Terracotta Horse and Rider, Ivory Thimble—don't tell me I'm wrong, but, dammit, they don't tell me that I'm right either. I'm back where I started, trying to focus a digital camera through the display glass.

I've found myself becoming obsessed by air space—the empty spot where blank happened—as if quantum history particles stay behind after an event or where someone actually stood. One time, with a photo as a guide, I counted the fence rails, the bricks, and took a picture of the window Marilyn Monroe leaned out of at the end of *The Seven Year Itch*. I've found all sorts of good mash-ups online—with the perspective just right, people have photoshopped the black-and-white pics with colour ones. It's cool, but there's not one bit of science to prove that talent, friendship, or memory can be claimed by standing on any invisible X.

I've toured the room where Edgar Allan Poe's young wife Virginia coughed her last sigh, and seen the bed that Lincoln was carried to after getting shot at a play. I'm the one who pisses off the tour guide with that question: "Which chairs specifically, or mirror, or bookshelf in this room were actually here when the Marquis de Lafayette slept here?" The guide is forced to admit that nothing in the room is original, though it's all period, apparently. Even the wallpaper and the position of the bed have been guessed at. *If we're done with questions*—glare—*please follow me down this corridor that we'll all pretend is not equipped with a fire extinguisher and a thermostat . . .*

With myself as tour guide, I've gone to addresses and streets with no plaques or statues to mark them. Like a private investigator on the tube or with a borrowed bicycle, I've knocked on a door or two. After interrupting dinner, the puzzled inhabitants even invited me in for a look around—don't mind the pile of laundry—the house where T. E. Lawrence wrote *Seven Pillars of Wisdom*. Climbing upstairs, it was like I'd finally tracked him down, like he'd be there scribbling words, filling the page from edge to edge with sentences. But, of course, he's not there, and he's not even just stepped out for tea. I've missed him by almost a century.

These nice people have lived here longer than he did and they'd like to finish their dinner.

A few years after I wrote *Mary's Wedding*, I got to finally visit Moreuil Wood. It's a battlefield without a memorial park, gift shop, or information centre. In the freshly turned soil, sloping up toward the wood, I picked out pieces of shrapnel and rusted artillery casings. Among the trees, without any spring leaves to hide them, I made out dips in the ground that were shell craters and slit trenches. Walking around the back corner of the wood, where C Squadron of the Lord Strathcona's Horse had ridden, I saw where they'd spotted the enemy. Here, Flowerdew gave his order, and his troopers drew their sabres and charged the German bayonets and machine guns. They fought here, or died there, or just a bit farther along maybe, but I couldn't be more exact, as if it mattered. I'd found the place I'd written about, but also, that it wasn't the place. A farmer stared at me from his tractor and a French Air Force fighter scorched across the sky. A Mirage—that's the name of the jet.

I think that I dramatize history in a frustrated effort to make it solid and real. I want the dead to live again, so that they'll walk and talk for me. I want to slow things down. And it seems important, for some reason, that I tell the audience that there were other people here before us. All of this is their air space—people lived in it, but not in the past, no, because the past doesn't exist. The past was a present that just happens to have occurred some time ago. Those famous folks whose work we like or don't, and the anonymous Josephs and Jaynes whose worst moments and favourite tunes are lost, were living the only now available to them. And although their now seemed permanent, it proved temporary, just like ours will.

What I want these paying customers with their cars in the parking lot to do with this reminder of the absurd state of their existence, I can't tell you. I mean, what can any of us do? Dance more often, eat more ice cream, or (wink) read more history? The clock can't be stopped for anyone, and though I'd hoped to maybe earn a pass, that includes me. It'll have to be enough that for tonight, on stage, that long-gone now and our now are the same now. We are them and they are us. Until the curtain call. After that, when the theatre goes dark, history does what it does, retreating to graveyards, museum archives, or back into unread books that are out of print. Most likely it ghosts away farther than that, somewhere between the lines, or so far off the edge of the page that words no longer help.

Stephen Massicotte
March 8, 2016

ACKNOWLEDGEMENTS

Mary's Wedding was written and developed with the assistance of the Alberta Foundation for the Arts, the Alberta Playwrights' Network, the Workshop West Playwrights' Theatre Springboards New Play Festival, and the 2000 Banff Playwrights Colony—a partnership between the Canada Council for the Arts and Alberta Theatre Projects. Thanks to Vanessa Porteous, Bob White, Ron Jenkins, and Gina Wilkinson for so thoughtfully guiding the play to its premiere.

Captain S. H. Williams's book *Stand to Your Horses*, a history of the Lord Strathcona's Horse (Royal Canadians) in the First World War, was an invaluable historical resource. In addition, the staff of the Military Museums of Calgary were always gracious with their personal attention, and on several occasions granted special access to the collections.

This third edition comprises the text of the tenth anniversary production at Alberta Theatre Projects. Thanks to Bob White and Dina Epshteyn for their careful dramaturgy on this "re-opening" of the play. Thanks to Playwrights Canada Press, and especially Annie Gibson and Blake Sproule, for agreeing to publish it (again).

A special thank you to Dina Epshteyn for her ongoing support and editorial expertise.

STEPHEN MASSICOTTE was born in Trenton, Ontario, and spent his earliest years living on various Canadian Forces bases in Canada and Europe. For the most part, he grew up in Thunder Bay, where he developed his interests in reading, film, and art. He studied graphic design at Cambrian College, and later, theatre at the University of Calgary. After graduating with a BFA in Drama, he stayed in Calgary to work as an actor, helping to found Ground Zero Theatre and The Shakespeare Company. With the Fringe Festival circuit success of his play, *The Boy's Own Jedi Handbook*, Stephen began to focus on playwriting. In 2002, *Mary's Wedding* premiered at Alberta Theatre Projects and has gone on to have more than a hundred productions in Canada, the US, New Zealand, and the UK. In the years following, Stephen has continued to write for the theatre, as well as opera, film, and fiction. His play *The Oxford Roof Climber's Rebellion* is the winner of the Gwen Pharis Ringwood Award for Drama at the Alberta Literary Awards and the Carol Bolt Award for Drama. *The Clockmaker* won a Betty Mitchell Award for Outstanding New Play and the inaugural Toronto Theatre Critics' Association Award for Best Canadian Play. He currently lives in New York City.

Third edition: April 2016. Second printing: July 2020.
Printed and bound in Canada by Marquis Imprimeur, Montreal

Cover photo copyright © 123RF
Author photo © Dina Epshteyn

PLAYWRIGHTS CANADA PRESS
202-269 Richmond St. W.
Toronto, ON
M5V 1X1

416.703.0013
info@playwrightscanada.com
playwrightscanada.com